TWISTED DESIRE: IN TOO DEEP

Printed in the United States of America

Grateful acknowledgements:

Cover design: J. Rene Creative

Editor: Tanisha Stewart

Beta Reader and Proofreader: LaKesha DeBardelaben

AISN 9798294767327

Contents

Chapter 1
The Garden of Eden

They call me Eden. The new girl with the short black dress and the ass that makes men tip double just to tap it to see if it's real. And it is! My real name is Nia Daniels. Detective Nia Daniels, from the Detroit Police Department, if you wanna be proper about it. But here in the Echelon nightclub, Damien Bishop's rooftop playground above the city lights, I'm Eden. I wear an 18-inch black wig with brown highlights, lashes, and a little gold name tag that says *Ask Me About Bottle Service* while I watch rich men break laws, get drunk, and drop stacks like its nothing.

I'm supposed to be invisible. That's how undercover works. You get close enough to smell the rot but never let it stick to your skin. But with Damien, it sticks.

I feel him the second he walks in. It doesn't matter if it's 10:00 p.m. or 2:00 in the damn morning. The bass could be shaking the walls, the girls could be half-naked dancing on tables, but when Damien shows up, the room shifts. He's not even boisterous about it. He enters the room with a black silk shirt, diamond chain, and Creed cologne. I swear it follows me home when I strip my uniform off at dawn.

Damien Bishop grew up on the hard edge of the city, with no father and a mother working three jobs to make ends meet; a hunger for power that started with corner hustles and small street deals. He clawed his way up from nothing, turning small-time drug runs into a multi-million - dollar empire. My department says he's ruthless. His soldiers say he's soft if you're loyal and deadly if you're not. They say he built his entire empire with dirty money and secrets nobody dares to repeat.

I'm here to prove they're right. Get close. Get the files. Get the evidence. And get the hell out. Easy plan, huh? Except I hate how I feel when he looks at me. He undresses me with his eyes, and that makes my panties wet.

Tonight's party is bigger than usual. Word is a Grammy-winning rapper's in VIP. The bottle girls keep dropping trays because they're too busy videoing themselves on Instagram. The DJ — Tanner, who's technically my partner when he's not pretending to be half-drunk behind the booth, winks at me when I pass by with my tray balanced on my shoulder.

"Smile, Eden," he mouths over the music. I flip him off behind my back, but I do smile just how Damien likes his pretty things.

I catch him tonight on the second floor, by the gold railing, his crew surrounding him like security but not too close. He's got a glass of something dark in his hand, the ice catching the strobe lights. He's talking to some NBA player, but his eyes are on me.

My stomach does that stupid flutter I hate. I remind myself what he is and who I am.

An hour later, the lights come up. The guests stumble out to the valet for their Escalades, Denalis and Porsches. The girls switch from bottle service to sneaking leftovers into to-go cups. I'm behind the bar, wiping sticky counters, counting my tips that are more than a week's salary on my real job.

The girls are gone and I'm folding the last pile of napkins. I don't hear him come up behind me. He doesn't clear his throat. He just appears, all that quiet danger wrapped in a silk shirt and gold.

"You're always the last one to leave?" His voice slides down my spine like honey.

I keep my eyes on the black cloth napkin in my hand. "Somebody's gotta make sure you don't wake up to sticky floors and bad Yelp reviews."

He laughs low, warm, just enough to show me he doesn't laugh for everybody. He sets a bottle of Paul Masson on the counter next to my elbow and grabs two brandy glasses.

"Sit with me a minute, Eden."

It doesn't feel like an order. It feels like an invitation I should turn down, but I don't. This can be my opportunity to get some intel.

Chapter 2

Just One More Drink

I tell myself it's just one drink. One drink to keep him comfortable and talking to me. One drink to keep the walls soft enough so he can learn to trust me.

Damien pours slowly, two fingers of brandy, no ice. He slides the glass across the bar to me, as if he's done this a thousand times before. But he's not looking at the glass. He's looking at me like I'm the thing he wants to taste.

I swirl the liquor gently in my glass, take a sip, and lick my lips so sensually, I'm sure his mister is rising. "Umm...smooth," I say, looking him up and down with my big brown eyes. I shake my hair and cross my legs. His gaze falls on my D-cup breasts. "You always drink with your staff?" I ask, just to keep my mouth moving so I don't do something stupid like kiss him.

He shrugs, that lazy half-smile playing at the corner of his mouth. "Not usually. You're special."

I snort, because I don't know what else to do with the way he says it. "You don't even know me."

His eyes leave my bosom and move lower to my legs and thighs. Yeah, he wants me. He's flipping through pages I didn't give him permission to read.

"Where are you from?" he asks as he sits next to me, sipping his brandy. I lie, but sprinkle in some truth to keep a straight face. I'm a single mom from the South Side of Chicago. I learned to hustle early, leaving home at seventeen when I got pregnant. I was in love, you know. Probably should have listened to my parents. "My baby daddy left as soon as Zaria was born." I finish, and then my mind goes dark. He was actually fucking the bitch down the street while I was giving birth, but what I told him was good enough. Everything was true except my baby died three days after she was born from birth asphyxia.

He rubs my arm. "Baby girl, that's fucked up!" He pours more brandy into my glass.

I move to a leather chair. He tells me about his grandmother, Gloria Bishop, like I don't already have her obituary pinned in a file in my office. He brags about his mother and then talks about stealing a box of bootleg CDs from the trunk of a local CD/DVD seller's car when he was sixteen and flipping them on the block for triple. Damien sighs and lowers his voice when telling me about losing friends and family to the streets, and how money doesn't fix the holes it leaves behind. He's telling me all about the juvenile criminal behavior, but I need more than this to help build this case.

"Money's just armor," he says, rolling his glass between his palms. "Keeps the right people out, keeps the wrong ones close. Remember that," he says, giving me a wink before taking another sip.

I'm supposed to hate him. He's feeding me exactly the kind of line that keeps girls hot and horny in his bed and loyal enough not to talk. But he's not saying it like a line to me. He's saying it like he wants me to have a come-up in life. Damn him to hell! And that's the part that scares me more than any threat in my handler's file.

One drink turns into two. I'm laughing before I realize it. Yeah, I have a buzz going on right now. He's telling me a story about setting his uncle's car on fire for the insurance money back in '02. I'm tipsy, not sloppy, but infatuated enough that when his knee bumps against mine, I don't pull away.

"I should. I really should," I whisper.

"What did you say?" he asks.

"Nothing." I force myself alert.

"You tired?" he asks. His voice is softer now. We're in this empty club. It's just us and the ghosts of a hundred secrets soaked into the walls and leather chairs.

I roll my eyes and push my hair back behind my ear. "My feet are killing me."

"Come here."

Two simple words. So dangerous. He pats the space between his knees.

I don't think. I slide out of my chair and step closer to him, my thighs brushing against his. He lifts my right foot, slips my heel off like he's unwrapping a present. His hands are warm and firm against my ankle, and he is performing a deep tissue massage on my feet and ankles.

"Do you always take girls' shoes off, Mr. Bishop?" I try to joke, but my voice cracks halfway through.

He lifts his eyes, one corner of his mouth curving just enough to make me feel stupid and special at the same time. "Only the ones I want to stay around."

I can't breathe. My pulse is thumping so loud I'm sure he can hear it. I should pull back and call it a night. Instead, I lean in. Just a little, and open my legs a little wider. Just enough for him to take a glance at my purple lace panties.

His hand slides up, palm warm on the back of my knee. My skin tingles under his rings. He smells of brandy, Creed, and desire. That damn cologne is gonna haunt my sheets tonight.

"I should go," I whisper, but my hips shift closer all on their own.

"You should," he murmurs, brushing his nose against my jaw. "But you won't."

I'm so drawn to him. I kiss him full throttle, my tongue is dancing in his mouth. I'm not thinking about the case. At this point, I couldn't care less about that damn badge. I needed to do this just once. I'm taste testing, and he tastes so damn good. His mouth is warm, patient, like he's waiting to see if I mean it. When I do it again, he answers with his tongue slow and deep, one hand sliding around my waist like he's steadying me, so I don't fall apart right there between his legs.

One second, we're kissing, the next I'm half sprawled across the brown leather chair. He lifts me like I weigh nothing, sets me down right on the soft royal blue Bubble 2-Curve sofa.

His hands slip under my dress. My thighs open like they've been waiting for this since the first day I clocked in. I'm feeling a shortness of breath. He's too busy kissing my inner thighs to notice.

When he pushes inside me, it's slow like he wants to feel my pussy stretch around every inch of his dick. Like he wants to memorize exactly how I open up for him, tight, slick, hungry.

He folds me over the sofa like a cheap folding chair, one hand pressing the back of my neck down, the other gripping my hip so hard I know I'll feel it tomorrow.

He doesn't bother with sweet talk; he doesn't need to. He flips me onto my back and watches my mouth fall open when he sinks deeper, and my thighs shake when he drags it out slow, then slams back in so deep I have to bite my bottom lip to keep from screaming.

"Damien," I moan, when he grinds in deep and rough. My pussy clenches so hard around his dick, I swear I see stars. My nails dig into his upper back, scratching lines that'll be there long after we break this case.

When I come, it's messy as hell. My back arches, and my ass is pressed against his hips while he licks my cheek and curses low in my ear. "This is the best dick you'll ever have. Baby, open your legs wider and take every inch of it."

"Is it nice and wet for you, baby?" I ask, barely catching my breath.

"Hell, yeah!" he says, grinding and smacking my voluptuous derriere.

"Don't... don't stop!" I scream at the top of my lungs.

He pulls my hips back harder, like he's fucking the last of my good sense out of me.

When he climaxes, it's a broken growl, his teeth on my shoulder, his dick buried so deep inside my pussy I swear I will feel it for days after the case is sent to the District Attorney's office. He stays pressed to my back for a second, breathing heavily, hands still holding me down like I'm the only thing he owns anymore.

And the worst part is, I want him to own me like this again and again, until there's nothing left to confess but his name. Damien.

After, I sit there on the sofa, totally relaxed and satisfied. He takes my panties and puts them in his pocket, then pours me another drink with the same steady hands that just ruined me. We don't say much. We don't have to. He looks at me like he knows this wasn't just sex, and I look back like I'm terrified he might be right.

Chapter 3
The Office

It's been a week since Damien made me forget every rule I swore I'd follow. Since I let the man I'm supposed to bust break me wide open instead. I tell myself I'm only here for the job. I repeat it like a prayer every night when the bass rattles the glasses and Damien's eyes find mine across the room.

But tonight isn't about Damien's stare or the way his smile makes my knees go soft. Tonight, I'm hunting. It's two in the morning when the last drunks stumble out. The kitchen is empty; the bar is shut down. The girls count their tips near the exit, squealing over cash while the bouncers pretend not to listen. I wave them off with a tired grin, wait until the big door thumps closed, then slip down the hall toward Damien's private office.

His office door is always locked, and tonight, it's cracked. Only a select few have access to his office, but only when he is present. Did a rookie make a big mistake, or is it bait? I pull a glove from my apron pocket and slowly push it open, my head peeks inside before I dare to enter.

I closed the door behind me. Inside, it smells like him. I can't get distracted. I spot the safe tucked behind a shelf, just like Tanner said it would be.

I drop to my knees and tug the shelf aside. My heart's banging so loud I swear it echoes off the wood floors. I tap in the numbers one by one, counting the soft beeps, flinching at every tiny beep in the dark. And then, click, click. I'm in.

Shit, I hear his voice low, clipped, and getting closer. He's on the phone, and from the sound of it, he's pissed. I've got maybe ten seconds. I slam the safe shut, muscle the bookshelf back into place, peel off the gloves and stuff them in my apron. I drop onto his oversized leather throne just as the handle jiggles. He walks in, and I'm sitting at the king's desk in the dark.

"Lose something, Eden?" he asks with a scowl on his face.

His voice slices straight through me; the hair on the back of my neck stands up. I jerk up so fast from that damn chair. Damien is standing in front of his desk, no smile this time, no undressing me with his eyes. The only light in the office comes from the soft glow of the hallway. I have to think of something quick.

"I thought you left the door cracked for me," I say, forcing a little laugh that feels like sandpaper. "I was sitting here waiting for..." My voice trails off and I giggle when he doesn't respond.

"You think that's funny?" he says, voice low and unnaturally calm. He turns around and shuts the door. Total darkness until he turns on the desk lamp.

"You know," he says, motioning me away from his chair. "Most girls knock when they want something from me."

I swallow. "Guess I'm not like most girls."

He crouches down in the chair, his gold watch glinting under the desk lamp. "I don't blame you, Eden. I just wonder what exactly you were planning to steal while you waited to get fucked again."

"Steal? No, baby, I steal hearts, not things," I say.

He opens his mouth with the tip of his tongue showing. "Sit your pretty ass down," he says, pointing at the big Lexington armchair behind me. "If you want to play in my office, you'll play by my rules."

He walks over to me, sexy and confident. I'm ready for an encore. His thumb softly brushes my jaw. He leans close to me and kisses my lips, and then he steps back.

"Go home, Eden," he says. "I have some business I need to take care of."

I dare not argue the point. I leave with nothing. No evidence. No orgasm.

***

Tanner jerks his chin. "Well?"

I shake my head. "Didn't get in. He found me there. I had to think quickly."

"Lucky you didn't get your cover blown, Daniels." Tanner flicks his lighter for his cigarette, the flame cutting across his pissed-off glare. "Sarge wants something solid tomorrow or she's pulling you out."

I slump into the passenger seat; the adrenaline burning out of my veins so fast it leaves me cold. I yank my burner phone from my pocket, thumb trembling on the screen. Two missed from Captain Johnson.

I call back, and she answers on the first ring.

"Daniels?" Her voice snaps like a whip. "Where the hell have you been? Tanner said you'd have something by tonight."

"I almost did," I mutter into the phone so low that my partner doesn't hear all of it. "The safe's real. The cash and the files are also in there. But he walked in and almost caught me. I couldn't risk blowing it."

"I'm not asking for 'almost,' Daniels. I'm asking for evidence. If Bishop's paying off judges or laundering cartel money through those weekend soirees, I need it now."

"I know, Captain," I snap. My pulse spikes again, the smell of Damien's cologne still clinging to my shirt. "I'll get it. I just need more time."

There's a pause. I hear her exhale; she's probably dragging on a cheap gas station cigarette, like always.

"You're getting sloppy. I've got half the brass up my ass wanting this case shut before the DA's office makes it someone else's collar."

"I'm not sloppy," I clap back. "I'm close. I just need him to trust me more."

"Then make him trust you. Make him need you. Make him desire you."

I laugh, but there's no humor in it. "Copy that, Captain."

She hangs up without another word.

Tanner glances at me from the driver's seat, flicking ashes out the window. "What'd she say?"

I lean my head back and close my eyes. "Same thing they always say."

"Which is?" he asks.

I lift slightly, peel open one eye, turn my gaze to him, lean my head back again with both eyes closed. "Get closer."

Chapter 4
The Surprise

The next morning, I tell myself I'm done. I can't afford to have another slip-up with him. Two is a pattern, and patterns get you killed in my line of work, or worse, get you reassigned to a desk where you spend your days filling out paperwork for rookies who don't know their asses from their feet. My phone rings.

"Hello," my voice hoarse from waking up.

"Eden, you have one hour to get dressed and wear something sexy."

"Damien, it's 9:20 a.m., and you want me to dress sexy?" I let out an audible yawn. "What do you have in mind?"

"Don't worry about it. I'm sending a driver to your home in an hour. Be ready."

He hangs up the phone. I drowsily walk to the bathroom and get in the shower, brush my teeth, and slip into my body-forming black catsuit and red stiletto heels. Apply my make-up with precision and call my sergeant and Tanner to inform them Damien is coming to my cover house to pick me up. They're happy to hear this and hope that I find something for the case.

An hour later, I step out of the building to find a sleek black car waiting at the curb. The driver greets me by name and opens the door with a slight nod. The ride is silent except for the hum of the city rolling by, and when we pull up, I realize I'm at The Townsend — the most luxurious hotel in Detroit. The doorman rushes to open the door for me, and inside, the lobby gleams with tiers of twinkling crystals and smooth, ivory-veined stone floors. Damien is waiting by the elevator, dark suit crisp, tie undone just enough to hint at the trouble he brings.

He doesn't speak, he takes my hand, guiding me to the penthouse. When the elevator doors slide open, I gasp. The entire suite is covered in rose petals, red and white, drifting across plush carpets and the massive king-sized bed. A small table by the window holds a glistening chocolate fountain surrounded by strawberries. Damien picks up a berry, dips it into the warm chocolate, and lifts it to my lips.

I part them slowly, teeth grazing the fruit as I bite down. Chocolate drips onto his finger, and without breaking eye contact, I lean in and suck the sweetness from his index finger, my tongue swirling around the tip of his finger until he lets out a low moan.

Damien pops the cork on a bottle of champagne like he owns the world, and right now, maybe he does. He pours a glass, the bubbles fizzing as he brings it to my lips. I take a sip, eyes locked on him, tasting the sweetness and the promise of what is to come.

He then lights a joint, rolls it slowly between his fingers before taking a long pull, eyes half-lidded as he exhales a cloud that smells like sin. There is smoke curling around my face as he murmurs, "I'm going to tear that pussy up. You keep this up, I ain't going to be studying those other bitches. You're the type of woman I'll take home to my mom."

"Damn, I don't know what to say. It's only been a month since we've known each other. Let me just tell you. I'm feeling you, too."

"You could be my woman."

The words send a hot shiver right through me. I lick the last of the champagne off my bottom lip, tasting his promise. I lean in so close our mouths almost touch, my breath brushing his. "I want you right now," I say, my voice low and dripping with need. "I want to ride your face until I come. And then I want more. All of it."

He just grins wickedly, hungry, and flicks the ash off the end of the joint. I know exactly what's about to happen, and I'm so damn ready to let him ruin me, one stroke at a time.

"I didn't want you in my office last night. That's why I told you to leave. I wanted to plan something special for you," Damien murmurs, his other hand stroking my cheek. "You're not a quick distraction to me, Eden. You're special. I can see this going somewhere if you'll let it."

I have tears in my eyes. "I don't know what to say, Damien."

He tilts my chin up, pressing his forehead to mine as his thumb traces my lower lip. The city stretches out behind us through the floor-to-ceiling windows, but all I see is him, and all he sees is me, temptation wrapped in a black catsuit and red heels. I'm ready to give him my body and my secrets.

Damien throws me onto the bed like he can't wait another second to have me. His hands slide down my legs, and he lifts one foot to his lips. He kisses each toe slowly, softly, and deliberately, like every inch of me deserves worship. He trails those kisses up my legs, pausing at my thighs, teasing me with every breath until he reaches my neck.

When his lips land there, he devours me. He sucks on my neck like he's starved for me, like I'm the only thing that can satisfy him. My body arches into his as I moan softly, already dizzy from his touch.

Then he moves back down to my breasts, his tongue swirling around one nipple while his hand fondles the other. He starts gently, licking and sucking with care to arouse me even more, but then his hunger shifts. His pace quickens. One moment he's tender, the next he's pulling at my nipple hard, making me gasp, then easing again. That push and pull makes my body tremble. Then, with a low growl, he pushes my breasts together and takes both nipples into his mouth at once. The sensation is overwhelming, hot, wet, and perfect. I need more of him.

My hips are rising off the bed. I reach for him, breathless. "Please," I beg, my voice trembling. "I want you inside me."

He grips his thick, long, hard dick, teasing my clit just long enough to make me whimper, moan, and groan. When he finally thrusts into me, it's slow, deep, and passionate, like he's claiming every inch of me. I wrap my legs around him, pulling him deeper, matching his rhythm with my own.

I'm popping my coochie, and he's begging me to tense my muscles when he goes in deep. "There it is, baby, I feel you, I hear you, give me all your love juice."

My leg is hooked over his shoulder, and my body is entirely his. The headboard is slamming the wall in rhythm with every rough, perfect thrust. Our bodies move together like we've done this a thousand times, like we were made for this moment. I feel every thick inch of him stretching me, filling me, driving me wild. The way he holds me tight and possessively makes me feel desired and owned in the best kind of way.

"Fuck, Eden..." he groans against my calf, his breath hot on my skin.

That sound alone pushes me closer. My nails dig into his back. My legs tremble. I'm clenching just like he likes it, pulling him deeper, chasing that high. And when I cum, it's an explosive wave of pleasure crashing through me, one after another, until I can't even think logically anymore.

He follows right after, burying himself inside me with a final deep thrust. His body jerks, then he releases it all into me as he groans my name repeatedly. He pulls out, and I lick the cum off his dick.

For a moment, we're both silent, breathing heavy, our bodies tangled and drenched with sweat. Then he slowly rolls off me, his arm staying wrapped around my waist as if letting go isn't an option. I turn to face him, and he brushes the hair from my face, his touch gentle now, like he's afraid I might disappear.

"I'm going to take care of you and your daughter," he whispers, voice husky and low.

I kiss him and lie on his chest. He has that power over me. I'm literally fucked in every way. We lay there, limbs intertwined, hearts still racing. No words needed. Just the quiet hum of connection and the heavy satisfaction of two bodies that have just shared something more than lust. This isn't just sex. It's something more. I fall asleep in his arms.

Chapter 5

Falling Hard

A month has passed, and somehow Damien has slipped into every part of my life like he was always meant to be there. What started with lust has turned into late-night talks, inside jokes, and the way he talks about my imaginary daughter like she's his own; makes me want to have his babies. It scares me how natural it all feels, how easily I let him in. But deep down, I know this shouldn't be happening. We were never supposed to fall for each other. I was supposed to be taking him down. Instead, I handed my heart over to him and fell deep in love.

Tonight, he takes me out to a quiet little restaurant downtown. I have on a casual outfit, but he looks at me like I'm drenched in all the diamonds he's given me. All I want is his heart. Over dinner, he can't stop touching me, his fingers brushing my thigh underneath the table, his eyes telling me I'm the only woman for him.

I'm enjoying every minute of our date, but the part that really catches me off guard is when he says casually, "There's someone I want you to meet after dinner."

My stomach tightens. "Okay, baby." Will I finally get the intel to take him down? I can't do this anymore. I don't want to arrest him. I want to be his lady. I'm totally screwed.

We leave the restaurant and drive in silence until we pull up to a modest house, where a warm light glows through the curtains. And when his mother opens the door, she pulls me into the kind of hug that says she's already heard everything about me.

"So this is the woman my son can't stop talking about," she says, smiling.

"Okay, Mama, that's enough. Don't give her the big head," he says, laughing, then kisses me on the cheek, pats my butt, takes my hand, and leads me into his mother's beautiful home.

He brags about me to his mother, then he says 'it.' "Mama, Eden is not just my girlfriend. I'm making her my right hand."

My head turned around towards him so fast. "Baby. What?!"

"You heard me. You're my lady, and you're too intelligent and motivated to be a bottle girl forever. Plus, with this power, no one dares to disrespect you."

My eyes are wide, and my jaw is on his mother's Egyptian rug. "What about Steve? He's been your right-hand for years?"

"And he will continue to be my right hand in certain areas of my business."

Okay, this is it. I'm in, but can I do this to the man I love? The man who treats me like a queen and handles me so tenderly? He's given up all the women for me. I love him so much. He gives me all his love. Love is an action word, and he shows his love every day. I've never felt like this before. I think about him when I go to bed and when I get up, and when we're together, I don't want him to leave. I feel lost when I'm not with him. Damn, what am I going to do?

After we leave his mother's, we walk under the stars, his hand wrapped tightly around mine. He stops walking and pulls me close, his forehead resting against mine. "I love you," he says, voice firm and sure. My heart skips a beat because I've felt it, but hearing it makes it all the more real.

"I love you, too," I say, looking into his dilated pupils. He kisses me so tenderly, like he wants to memorize the moment. And in that kiss, I feel everything: safety, heat, danger, and the truth. What am I going to do? This can't keep riding the fence.

We shouldn't be in love. There are too many lines crossed; there are too many reasons why this can't work. But in his arms, the rules don't matter. The world quiets down. And even if we're walking into something forbidden, we're walking into it together. Our hearts are on the line. And for the first time in a long time, I'm not afraid to be loved and to love that special person. But is he worth my career?

***

A few days later, I'm working on spreadsheets in his office. I can search since I have access to the office without him being in there, but I'm limited in what I can access.

I tell myself it's just another room in a man's empire that I'm paid to collect evidence on and report back to my squad. But when I slip the spare key card from Damien's office drawer, the one he thinks he hides so cleverly behind that stack of black leather notebooks, my hands tremble. I'm feeling sick to my stomach. I hate what I have to do.

Tanner's voice buzzes in my head. "You need to get what we need. I'm beginning to think you and that piece of shit are dating for real. What are you waiting for?" This is what I hear from him every day, and I'm sick of it.

I crouch down under the desk and use that keycard to open his secret drawer underneath the desk that he doesn't think anyone knows about. Of course, I peeped it. I'm a detective.

Tonight, he's downstairs working the room. Big-name execs, a famous producer from Atlanta, hush-hush chatter about a new artist he's about to launch — that we've kept a secret for months. I negotiated and got the best deal for the artist and a damn good deal for our company. I mean Damien's company. I've got maybe twenty minutes before someone notices I'm not on the floor.

There's nothing in this drawer I can use, but some people will be ready to kill him if they saw the potential blackmail pictures. Especially the congressman. I don't think I can look at him the same way again. I put the pictures back and replaced the key card in its hiding place.

I move the bookshelf and open the safe. I remembered the code from when I broke into it weeks ago. I start snapping pictures. Click. Click. Cash. Click. Bribes. Click. Hits on enemies, click, and tax fraud, click.

Each flash feels like a hand digging out my heart and soul. I sigh. This is not a good man, but I want him, and he is all mine. He has softened being with me. He wants us to have three kids so my imaginary daughter won't feel lonely. I shouldn't care. But I do.

I close the safe. The captain will pull me now that I have the evidence to take him down. The DA will get their indictment of Damien, and he'll know exactly who put the nail in his coffin. I text Tanner and tell him I have the evidence and I'm bringing him the phone. He immediately calls me. I don't answer. I just cry, trying not to let the tears burn through my lashes. Too late.

Chapter 6
The Time Has Come

D amien comes into the office before I can give Tanner the phone. I'm clearly not okay. My eyes are red and swollen from crying. He rushes to me.

"Babe, what's wrong? How can I help you?" he asks as he pulls me into his arms and holds me tight. "Eden, you know I'll do anything for you. Just tell me what you need from me."

I fall to my knees sobbing while in his arms. He gently picks me up and says, "It's you and me against the world, and I won't let anyone or thing hurt my, queen."

"It's Tanner. He said something to me about me not having Zaria, calling me a bad mother. I want you to fire him, but don't tell him why. I don't want him to know how much it hurt me."

"I'll beat the shit out of him."

"No," I say. "Tell him we found another DJ and he is to leave immediately. You know the bartender Chris is a part-time DJ. We can promote him."

"As you wish, baby. I will take care of his ass now. I mean, I will relieve him of his duties now."

He walks me over to the chair, pours me a glass of red wine, and kisses the top of my head.

"Stay here. I'll be back in a minute. I love you with everything in me."

I take a sip and nod. He leaves the office. I had to get Tanner away from here. I'm not ready to hand over the evidence. I love this man. I see what no one else sees. He has good in him. He was dealt the wrong hand growing up. He has enough money for us to disappear to Belize or anywhere in the world.

He returns twenty minutes later. "It's done. You will never have to deal with him again. I promise that I will always keep you safe."

I run into his arms and passionately kiss him. "Make love to me, Damien."

He presses me against the Romantic Gray Stained Wood Wall and kisses me back. The truth doesn't matter to me. I'm lying to myself harder than I've ever lied to him.

We don't even make it to the chair. He pushes me to the wall, and I'm facing the wall. He's behind me, pressed against me. His hands slide under my blouse, his palms caressing my breast. He spins me around, picks me up, and lays me on the floor. His palm slides up my spine, holding me down like he's daring me to deny how bad I want this. I rip my clothes off, leaving only my panties as the only piece of clothing on my body.

I slide my fingers into my panties and pleasure myself while looking dead into his eyes.

"You know what you're doing to me?" he murmurs.

He uses his teeth to gently pull my panties down to my ankles, and I kick them across the office. He gets on top of me and pushes himself inside of me. I almost scream from euphoria.

I have to bite my arm to keep from screaming. He pulls my hair back so he can watch my mouth open for him.

"Ain't no secrets in here, Eden. Not tonight."

When I come this time, it's different. I'll protect him at all costs.

Later, I sneak out to check on things downstairs while he sleeps on the floor, one arm slung over his eyes like he can't stand to see daylight creep in.

I've missed calls from Tanner and the captain. I really don't care. I'll think about all this tomorrow. Tanner knows something's up. I know him just as he knows me. When you've been partners as long as we have, you know more about the person than their loved ones. He's been my partner for five years, and he knows me. He knows that I've fallen for Damien.

***

The sun is rising and I'm lying in bed deciding my future. The phone rings. It's Tanner.

"Tanner."

"Good morning to you, too, Eden. What was that shit you orchestrated last night?"

"Don't good morning me. He decided to go with another DJ. If I had tried to talk him out of it, it could have blown my cover. So, don't come to me all hostile and shit."

"Keep your damn voice down," he snorts. "Half these fools know exactly what you're doing in there. The difference is, you forgot what side you're doing it for. We need to meet, and you hand over the phone, we'll pull you out today!"

"Well."

"Well, what? You got the photos, right?" he asks.

"Yes." I deleted the real evidence and just left the photos of the bribes. I can't take the man I love down. "Let's meet at our usual spot in thirty minutes."

"Make sure you show up, Detective Daniels. I feel like I need to remind you who you really are."

"I know exactly who I am. I'll be there." I hang up on him. I know who I am. I'm Damien's lady.

We meet at the spot and I give him the burner phone. Tanner scrolls through the pictures. "This is all you got? It will work. We can get others to flip. Good work. We're closing soon. Don't go back to the club or see him. Say you have the flu or something. One more week and we pull the plug."

I nod like a good detective should. But all I can see is Damien's eyes when he said, "I want you to stay with me forever." The way he touched my jaw was like he was forgiving me for sins I hadn't even confessed yet. I will not stay away from him.

Later that night, Damien finds me telling everyone to do a thorough cleaning. It's close to time for a health inspection. He drags me into his office, locks the door, and kisses me so deeply and lovingly, I drop my pen and checklist. Next clothes are dropping.

"Baby, take out your phone and record us. I want you to watch if your eyes ever stray."

"I'll do it because it will be fun. You don't have to worry about me straying. There are only three people I love in this world. My mama, you, and my daughter I hope to meet when you say the time is right."

I look deep into his eyes, reaching his soul. "I know. Now start the recording."

We make love on his desk this time to smooth music by Maxwell. He pulls my hair back, sucks my neck, and whispers in my ear. "Move in with me."

This is it. The point of no return. "Yes," I say, losing all sense.

"Have you ever thought about leaving this place?" he asks, voice quiet, eyes on mine like he wants an answer I can't give him.

"Where would I go?" I ask.

"Anywhere but here. I don't want this life anymore. I want a family. A family with you. We will have enough money; we couldn't spend it all in a lifetime."

And I know that if he asks me to run, I'd follow. Badge be damned.

Chapter 7
The Mole

I feel it before I hear it — that shift in the air when something poisonous leaks into the room. The club's still loud, bass thumping through the walls like a heartbeat, but there's an edge tonight. The regulars watch each other too closely. The security crew whispers in the corners of the club, where they used to laugh and joke.

"They know." His voice is tight, no jokes now. "Somebody's feeding Damien rumors. Somebody told him he's got a mole."

A mole. I should feel insulted. I'm not a mole, I'm a detective. Detective Nia Daniels, Narcotics and Vice. Except I haven't felt like her in weeks. I feel like Eden. And Eden's about to drown with him if I don't run.

Damien's not in his usual spot when I slip into the back hallway. He's not in the office either. I find him on the second-floor balcony, glass in hand, leaning against the gold railing like a king watching the wolves circle.

He doesn't look surprised when I show up behind him. He just flicks his eyes over his shoulder, takes a slow sip, and says, "Got something you wanna tell me, Eden?"

I freeze. Part of me wants to lie, spin it slick, play dumb, and blame the other girls. But there's no point. He's not asking for the truth. He already knows.

I step closer to him with tears in my eyes. "Who told you?"

He laughs quietly and humorlessly. "Does it really matter?"

I reach for his arm. He lets me, but his body remains still as stone under my fingers. "Damien, I..."

He cuts me off with a look. It's not anger that kills me. It's the hurt in his eyes as he looks at me broken-hearted.

"You fuck me," he says, voice flat, "you smile for me, you run your mouth like you're loyal, but you got a badge shoved up under that tight little dress, huh?"

I flinch. He's not yelling, but I almost wish he would. Yelling means you care enough to fight. Silence means you're done.

"It wasn't supposed to go this far," I say, and my voice is trembling from the anguish I'm feeling right now.

"I love you. I didn't provide them with enough evidence about you. Just enough for a couple of years."

Damien tips the rest of his drink over the balcony; the amber drops vanish into the lights below. He turns back to me, really close now. He puts one hand on my throat, not squeezing, just there. Reminding me of whom I betrayed.

"You gonna take me down, Eden?" he murmurs. "Put me in a cage for the rest of my life?"

My breath catches. "I don't want to, and I made it so that you will hardly get any time. I'm willing to give my badge up for you."

We stand like two statues frozen under the strobe lights. My partner's blowing up my phone in my pocket. Urging me to get out now.

But I don't move. I'm not leaving my man.

His hand slides up from my throat to my jaw. The same spot he always touches when he's about to make love to me.

"You love me?" he asks. It's not soft. It's a dare. A bullet with my name on it.

I swallow the truth like poison. "Yes."

Then he kisses me. Hard. Messy. Nothing tender about it, just teeth and tongue and the taste of Brandy and bad decisions.

He breaks it first, breathing hard, forehead pressed to mine. "Then run, Eden. Run before I change my mind."

Behind him, two of his muscles stand on the stairs.

But all I see is Damien, the man I came to destroy, the man who destroyed me first.

I run. I don't look back. Not because I'm scared he'll come after me. But because I'm afraid he won't.

Chapter 8

The Broken Promise

The raid kicks off at 2:07 a.m., just late enough that the last rounds are poured, just early enough that half the club's too drunk to know what the black vans and plain suits mean.

I'm in the alley behind Echelon when it starts. Tanner's hand wraps around my wrist so tight my bones grind together.

"Get in the damn car, Nia," he snaps. No more Eden now and I'm back to my real name, whether I want it or not.

I pull my arm away. "He's still inside."

Tanner curses so loudly that it echoes off the brick wall. "Yeah? And when those doors burst open, he'll see who put him there. You wanna watch his face when they drag him out? You wanna be the badge he spits at on the way to the van?"

I want to say no. I want to say I'm not the reason. But I am. My fingerprints are all over the safe, the phone, and the files. My name is stamped on the warrant like a coffin nail.

Sirens scream from the front entrance, muffled over the bass still thumping through the walls. Red and blue lights paint the alley with my guilt and regret.

Tanner grabs my shoulders, shakes me hard enough that my teeth click. "Nia. Focus. You got your evidence. You did your job. Now leave."

But my feet won't move. Because somewhere behind that door is Damien Bishop, the man who pressed me up against a bar, a wall, a promise I was never supposed to keep. And he's about to watch the whole empire fall because I couldn't keep my heart out of my badge.

I see him before he sees me, through the side exit, half-shadowed by security who don't know yet that they're seconds away from handcuffs and mugshots. He's calm. Of course he is. His eyes flick over the scene, the flashing lights, plainclothes detectives flooding his nightclub. Then his gaze lands on me.

It's so fast like my whole chest folds in on itself. He doesn't yell, run, or fight. He just stands there in his white shirt half-buttoned, chain catching the alley light, looking at me like he's memorizing my face for the lonely nights in his jail cell.

Tanner drags me toward the car. I'm half-sobbing, half-cursing, my badge clinking in my pocket like thirty pieces of silver.

Damien's eyes never leave mine. Not when they cuff him. Not when they shove his head down to squeeze him into the back of a cruiser. Not when my sergeant nods at me like I'm some good dog who finally brought the damn bone home.

He doesn't say a word. He doesn't have to. The look is enough: You were mine. Now you're just a badge. And he's partially right.

The car door slams shut. Tanner accelerates out of the alley, tires screeching over my broken heart and promises. The club shrinks in the side mirror, but not my memories.

My hands shake in my lap. The cuffs. The keys. The photo I kept of him is tucked between my bra and my heart like a woman who lost the love of her life. I threw everything away tonight.

Chapter 9

A Slight Of Hand

Six weeks later, I'm back in my real uniform. Detective Nia Daniels, the undefined cop who closed the case, hero badge polished for the press. They say my name like it means something around here.

Bishop's investigation turned out exactly as they wanted: headlines, a perp walk, and three more indictments based on the evidence I fed them piece by piece, between drinks, kisses, and lies.

Damien sits behind reinforced glass now. Cell block A. No bail. His lawyer barely bothers to pretend. The DA is building a case out of my testimony. They say 'slam dunk' so much, I want to scream.

Tanner's the only one who knows the truth that it wasn't a slam dunk. It was a betrayal with lipstick on it. He stops me after the third closed-door briefing, corners me by the water cooler like we're still twenty-two and hungry to climb the ranks.

"You check your mail yet?" he asks, voice low.

I snort. "Fan letters from reporters?"

He shakes his head. "No, Nia. From him. He has your address. The captain isn't taking any chances. Officers are being sent to your house to protect you in case he makes a move from jail."

There's a knot in my throat, tension in my body, and my stomach feels nauseous. Then I realize that despite everything, I know in my heart, he would never hurt me. But wait a damn minute!

"How did you know he sent me a letter?" I ask, my voice rising.

"The warden contacted us to give you a heads-up. A new jailer put the letter in the mail, not knowing you were the detective who brought him down. He called the station today when he found out. The letter was mailed three days ago."

That makes sense, I tell myself. I assure Tanner I'll check for it and be safe, then I hang up. A plain envelope. But the second I see the handwriting, my mind drifts back to those nights when we lie in bed holding each other, talking, and laughing. He promised me that he would love me and protect me for the rest of my life.

Inside is a note. Eleven words. Written in that steady, clean script that used to scribble my name across bar napkins at 2:00 a.m. We're not done. Not even close. What we had was real.

I read it twice. I should throw it away, but I don't. Because part of me knows what nobody else does, he loves me, and he would never hurt me.

Internal Affairs asks if I want protection. I say yes, so they don't get suspicious.

I stand at my kitchen window that night, staring out at the street that suddenly feels too quiet. The badge on my table glints under the shitty overhead bulb. The same badge I traded my heart for. I swear I can feel him even locked behind concrete and steel, longing for me.

At the beginning, I wanted him caged, until I learned and fell in love with the real Damien. Now, I'm the one who can't sleep or breathe without him.

I call his lawyer and tell him to ask his client about a recording he has on his phone of him having sex with the undercover detective who brought him down. I hang up.

Why did I do that, one may ask? Because I know this isn't over. He loves me and I love him.

And when he gets out, and he will, he's coming for everything I didn't give him the first time. The truth and my unconditional love for him. I wonder if he will be angrier with me because he fell in love with my imaginary daughter.

I whisper it to the empty kitchen, a secret I can't file, a truth I can't testify to:

"Damien Bishop owns me and we will be together soon. I'm making sure of that."

The End ... For now...

Chapter 10
About the author

Geletta Shavers is a social worker, mental health therapist, and author who uses her voice to empower, provoke, and sometimes terrify. Known for chilling stories that burrow deep into the human psyche, Geletta blends real-world emotional insight with supernatural suspense in *Dragged Into Darkness*. Her years in mental health give her a rare perspective on fear, trauma, and survival — themes that pulse through every page.

In addition to writing spicy romance, horror and thrillers, Geletta created a powerful self-care journal for women under her pen name, Ms. G, LCSW. Whether guiding women toward healing or pulling readers into dark fictional worlds, she believes in the power of storytelling to confront the truth and sometimes, to escape it.

Other titles by Geletta Shavers include *The Inheritance of Amaya Montgomery, Loving Myself First: My Self-Care Journal. Dragged into Darkness, and a spicy romance-Twisted Desire: In too Deep.*

If you would like to connect with me, please visit www.gelettashavers.com. I would love to hear from you.

Instagram: author_geletta_123

YouTube: Geletta Shavers, LCSW

https://www.facebook.com/profile.php?id=61564210504377

Made in the USA
Columbia, SC
20 January 2026

77756298R00024